THE GIMMEL GANG

The Secret in the Basement

THE GIMMEL GANG

The Secret in the Basement

By Calanitte Kir-on

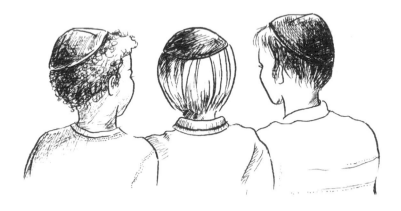

First impression November 2002
Printed in Israel

Computerset and cover design:
Geronimedia Ltd. Productions
98a Herzl Blvd
Jerusalem, Israel

Tel: 972-2-6515903
Fax: 972-2-6523532
Website: www.geronimedia.com
Email: info@geronimedia.com

Illustrations: Shuli Menachem

Distributed by:
Israel Book Shop
501 Prospect Street
Lakewood, NJ 08701

Tel: (732) 901-3009
Fax: (732) 901-4012
Email: isrbkshp@aol.com

Contents

In memory of all the soldiers and fellow Jews who have passed away as a result of bombings, in Israel and other places such as the Twin Towers. They died for Kedushat Hashem and will not be forgotten

To my dear brother, Ilan עמו"ש for giving me the Idea of the Gimmel Gang - unintentionally...

Foreword

"Where could he be? He's been gone all day and now we'll miss our flight!" Sara Rubin asked while pacing the floor of the hotel room frantically.

"I think it's time we called the police. It's just not like him to disappear like this," she added while picking up the phone and dialing the Denver Police Department.

That was two months ago. The Rubins, back home in Cleveland, Ohio (they returned home in case he looked for them...), were losing hope of ever seeing their little Daniel again.

They had spent a week together in Denver on a business trip that Mr. Rubin took. On the last day of the trip, their son Daniel left the hotel to take a walk and didn't return. The police tried very hard to find him but came up with nothing. The Rubins hired people to put up reward posters everywhere, but no one called in with any real information.

Where was he? What happened to Daniel?

CHAPTER 1 – DANIEL

"*Kabed es ovicho ve'es imecho...*" (Honor your mother and father). He thought again with tears streaming down his face.

"Will I ever find my parents again? Will I ever remember who they are? Who I am?" the boy wondered for what seemed like the millionth time.

Then he went to lie down on the old, beat up sofa in the hidden room at the back of the basement of the Denver Orthodox Boys' School. Pulling the curtain that he used as a blanket tighter around him, he started thinking about how he ended up in this musty, old room.

He had woken up and found himself in a strange place. All over and around him were bits and pieces of wood and debris. But before he really noticed this, his first thought was... "OW!" as he rubbed the bump on his aching head.

When he could gather enough strength to look around, he found that he was lying in a pile of rubble alongside a very quiet road. All around him were the remains of a building site under construction. It had collapsed just as he was exploring the area. Large pieces of wood had fallen down on and all around him, almost covering him up.

Daniel had no recollection of any of this. He had no idea whatsoever where he was or how he had gotten there. The scariest thing was when he realized that he had no clue of who he was. The only thing he knew was that he was Jewish. Not only because he was wearing a *Yarmulke* and *tzitzis*, but he also felt it in his heart.

He had brushed himself off as best as he could and slowly started pushing the loose boards aside as he climbed out of the mess. At last he was out and he started walking.

Now, he figured that the first place to go would be to a police station. Maybe they could help him find out who he was and where he came from. Along the way he kept looking around hoping to find something familiar, but sadly enough, he recognized nothing - not even one building!

A short distance ahead, he saw a park and thought he would rest there. He crossed the park until he found a bench and sat down. While he was resting, a woman and her son came and sat down next to him. They were chatting away when the boy stopped his mother to ask her a question. He was looking at a big building across the park, where a lot of children of different ages were running around, playing, sitting or reading.

"Mom," he asked.

"Yes," she answered, smiling down lovingly at him.

"What's that building?" he asked, pointing.

A sign nearby read "City Orphanage".

"It's a special orphanage" the mother replied.

When the young boy then asked what an orphanage was, the mother said, "Well, that's where the city places children who can't find their parents. They live there until someone comes to take them into their home."

That was all that Daniel needed to hear to make him panic. "Oh no!" he thought. *"If I go to the police, they'll put me in that orphanage and then a non-Jewish family might adopt me!"* He got up and started running as far away from the orphanage as he could. "I must hold on to my Judaism!" he whispered desperately to himself.

For the rest of that day, until late in the afternoon, Daniel had wandered around Denver wondering what he would do, when suddenly something caught his eye.

Across the street was a school with a sign on it that read, "Denver Orthodox Boys' School".

"A Jewish school!" he thought excitedly. He ran across the street and began checking out the school grounds. It was summer break so the school appeared to be deserted and closed down. He checked all the windows, but they were locked tight. As he circled the school once more, he looked up to the second floor and saw that one window was slightly open. He looked all around and when he felt sure that no one was looking, he climbed up a nearby tree. As he was climbing, Daniel froze in his tracks when he felt his *tzitzis* being pulled. He looked down and to his horror, saw that one of his *tzitzis* strands caught on a branch and tore. Cautiously, he continued to make his way along the ledge outside the windows until he reached the open one. He pushed it open and climbed inside. For the next hour he toured the school, delighted to find food in the kitchen with such delights as packaged cakes, cookies and crackers. He also found a spare *siddur* and pair of *tzitzis* (which he now needed to replace his torn and unkosher pair), in one of the classroom closets. He took them, but he promised himself that he would return them as soon as he could.

Daniel then went down to the basement, and after scaring away two mice, did a thorough examination of the enormous area. He had to find a place where he could hide, since he knew that until he could figure out what to do, he had nowhere else to stay.

Just as he was moving aside some shelves, he found the solution! An old, rusty door stood along the wall behind the shelves, and judging by the looks of the cobwebs everywhere, it had not been moved in ages. He tried the handle, and after jerking it and bashing his arm at the same time into the door, it gave way and opened.

"Wow!" he exclaimed. He suddenly found himself inside a room, with a beaten-up old sofa, a table, a chair and some shelves. It even had a lamp that just needed a light bulb. He looked all around and mumbled to himself, "It will have to do for now."

Later that evening, he explored more of the school and found a well-stocked library. *"Excellent!"* he thought. *"Now, at least, I can study Torah while I'm here."* It was then that he realized that by some miracle, even though he couldn't remember who he was, he could still remember how to learn quite easily. A voice inside him began saying the *"Modim"* passage said in the *Shemoneh Esrei*. *"Al Nissechah shebechol yom imonu…"* (for your miracles that are with us every day) he then said aloud with a sad smile. He carefully looked at the books and made sure to only take those that had copies and were old and ragged-looking. He was hoping that if someone happened to come into the school library to get a book or something, they wouldn't notice that anything was missing.

Daniel took the books and some food into the secret room and studied and *davened* for the rest of that day.

The next day, when he woke up, he hoped to have a plan of what to do next, but sadly nothing came to mind. Somehow, one day of hoping and praying led to another day and poor lost Daniel ended up staying in the boys' school for two months.

"I'm still here, with no memory of who I am" he thought to himself, as tears rolled down his thin cheeks. Although he took a bit of food from the school kitchen, he tried not to take too much and as a result, he lost a lot of weight.

Daniel looked at his watch and jumped up off of his "bed" when he saw that it was time to *Daven* (pray) *Minchah* (the afternoon service).

CHAPTER 2 – 'A THIEF WITH A HEART'

"I called you all here for a very important meeting." Rabbi Kaplan announced to the teachers as soon as they were all seated and settled down.

Rabbi Eliyahu Kaplan was the principal of the Denver Orthodox Boys' School, the school that the famous Gimmel Gang attended. Principal for 20 years and Rabbi of the East Side Orthodox *Shul* (Synagogue), Rabbi Kaplan was well known and loved by everyone. Even the non-Jewish people that met him or dealt with him couldn't help but admire him. He was always so kind, patient and understanding. Whenever people upset him, he kept his true feelings and opinions to himself so as not to arouse anger *Chas Veshalom* (Heaven forbid) in anyone. The students all felt very lucky to have Rabbi Kaplan as their principal, but there was one flaw with the Rabbi, you see. Rabbi Kaplan was *so* nice that whenever a boy was sent to him for punishment, all they needed was one of his kind yet disappointed looks and they would be in tears crying from guilt. Most of them never repeated their mistakes again.

"I would like to discuss the problem we've been having since the summer," Rabbi Kaplan began and then went on to explain.

"I'm referring to the *Sefarim* (holy books), the *tzitzis* and of course the food that has disappeared and continues to disappear from our school."

The teachers nodded their heads in understanding. This was no news to them, of course.

"We've all been trying to put it out of our heads since the police were here and came up with nothing," the Rabbi continued looking down at them with kind but very serious eyes.

"But I have called all of you here to try and see if somehow, together *we* can't catch this thief on our own. Do any of you have any thoughts or ideas on the matter? For instance – what is this thief doing with the *sefarim* that he steals?"

"Maybe he's selling them!" Rabbi Adler called out.

"I also thought that at first," Rabbi Kaplan answered. "But I don't think so anymore. You see, the books that were stolen, were all battered and torn books that had three or four other copies – NICE ones - right next to them. So if the thief wanted to make money, don't you think he would have taken those that were in better condition?"

The teachers all nodded their heads in agreement.

"Even the *pair of tzitzis* that was taken was old and stained and was lying around here as a spare for *years* now," Rabbi Kaplan added.

"You mean we have a thief with a heart, huh?" one of the teachers called out and several other teachers laughed at this.

"Well," said Rabbi Kaplan as he considered this, "something like that, I think."

"I have a feeling," he continued while rubbing his beard in thought, "that this is not your usual every day thief. No," he concluded, shaking his head in certainty, "if he were an ordinary thief, he would have stolen money, watches, wallets - things that are worth a lot more than what he's taken."

"So then what could it be?" the fourth grade teacher asked. "Why does he steal what he does and how can we catch him?"

"Well, I'm not sure," Rabbi Kaplan answered solemnly.

"I think we should all go home and give this some more thought. Tomorrow we'll see what other ideas we can come up with."

The meeting was over and the teachers all got up, pushed back their chairs, bid farewell to Rabbi Kaplan and left the room.

Meanwhile, three boys, who happened to be studying together after class in the nearby classroom, had overheard everything.

"Did you guys get all that?" Boruch Kahn asked his two best friends, Dovid Freedman and Meir Klein.

"Yeah..." the other two replied dreamily.

They were already doing what came naturally to them. They were trying to work out the mystery. Well, that's how the Gimmel Gang was.

Best friends since preschool, the boys had always done everything together, but it was the last summer that had changed their lives. They had helped their classmate and friend, Moishe Berenstein, catch the mailman who stole his family's special *mezuzah*. This *mezuzah* had been an heirloom of generations inherited by his mother. Ever since that episode, they were famous. Everyone in the Jewish community knew them and wherever they would go, people would whisper and talk about how brave they were. The Gang members, who were always so modest, just blushed and preferred not to be noticed. When kids asked them questions about the case, they usually just tried disappearing saying that they had class or something. Unusual for kids their age, they did *not* like to talk about themselves.

Suddenly, Dovid looked at his two friends with a wide grin on his face and said, "Guys... I think we have just found our next case!"

Boruch and Meir smiled, nodded their heads and said together, "Yep!"

"All right," Meir began, clapping his hands together. "We need a plan."

"Let's sit down and think for a minute," Dovid said as they sat back down at the table.

"Well," Meir began. "What do we already know? We know that the thief steals *sefarim*, food and in the past he stole a pair of *tzitzis* as well."

"Right," Dovid answered, concentrating very hard.

"And," Boruch stated, "he probably steals at night."

"Of course," Meir declared matter-of-factly. "When else would he do it?"

"But that's our biggest problem," Dovid told them. "I mean how can we spy on him at night? I can't really see our parents saying, (in his mother's voice) "Sure kids, go on and spend the night in your school… and have fun!"

The gang doubled over in laughter at the thought.

"So how CAN we catch the thief?" Meir asked.

"Well," Dovid replied in a very serious tone, "I say we do what we did last time."

"What did we do last time?" Boruch asked, confused.

Meir who caught on jumped up and said, "Excellent idea, Dovid!"

"WHAT IS???" Boruch asked, now a little upset that he didn't know what his two friends were talking about.

"Let's spend the next few hours, studying and saying *Tehillim (*psalms*)* until it's time to go home or until we come up with a good plan – which ever comes first."

"Oh-h-h-h!" said Boruch with a huge smile on his face, nodding his head in understanding.

And that's just what they did. They ran over to the library, borrowed some *sefarim* and brought them back to the room. They then set them down on the table and took their seats once again.

An hour and a quarter later, Boruch suddenly jumped up, hit his head with his hand as if to say, "how could I have missed this?" and shouted, "I've got it!"

He startled his two friends so much that they nearly fell out of their chairs!

"Got what?" they asked together looking up at Boruch, whose cheeks had turned bright pink with excitement.

"I have a plan and I *have* the plan," he replied with a very proud look.

"What are you talking about?'' the other confused boys nudged him.

"I've got a video camera!" Boruch proudly announced.

"That's perfect!" Dovid shouted.

"Yeah, we could hide it somewhere and film the thief in action!" Meir added excitedly.

The gang then talked about it and figured that the best place to hide the camera would be in the staff kitchen. This way they could film the thief taking food. Luckily, the camera had a tape that could record for twelve hours!

CHAPTER 3 – PLAN A

Once the boys finished studying, they each went home that day feeling very excited.

Boruch, of course, had a bit of pleading to do, but his parents were fairly used to his strange requests since the Berenstein mystery. He would never consider taking the camera without permission. Since his parents were well aware of the adventures and *mitzvos* of the "Gimmel Gang," and as long as Boruch completed his studies, and made sure there would be no danger involved, they let him do almost anything he wanted. Whenever Boruch had an unusual request, they asked their usual questions.

"What's it for? Is it safe?" and so on. When they were satisfied with the answers, they gave Boruch the video camera and showed him how it worked. They figured that even if the thief somehow found the camera, there was no way he could link it to them since there were no specific identification marks.

The next day, Tuesday, Boruch brought the video camera to school and showed it to Meir and Dovid.

"WOW!" the two boys exclaimed as they inspected the camera.

"Okay," Dovid then declared. "We have to set it up before the teachers all arrive."

Boruch and Meir then followed Dovid to the staff kitchen, and when they were sure no one was around Dovid and Meir began searching for a good place to put the camera. It had to be a place where it would remain unseen. Meanwhile, Boruch was peeking out of the door constantly to make sure no one would "surprise" them.

The boys looked all around, near the refrigerator, the cabinets, the counters, they even checked for enlarged mouse holes near the floor!

Meir was looking up at the cabinets nearest to the ceiling when he suddenly shouted, "Look, I've got it!" He was pointing high up at an air vent in the wall near the ceiling.

"Meir, you're a genius!" Dovid exclaimed patting his friend on the back.

"Thanks!" Meir answered feeling pretty good himself.

"But how are we going to get it up there?" Boruch asked.

"Well," Dovid said trying to come up with a plan. "Meir, why don't you climb on my shoulders and set the camera up behind the vent?"

"Hmm, I think I can." Meir answered while trying to hide the panic in his voice. He wanted to help so much that he didn't tell his friends about his fear of heights.

"Great!" Dovid exclaimed, walking over to Boruch to get the camera.

"Is it set? The timer and everything?" he asked Boruch as he handed him the video camera.

"It sure is!" Boruch answered proudly. "Good luck!"

Dovid then returned to stand near Meir and said, "Ready?"

"Uh, yeah," Meir answered forcing a smile.

Dovid kneeled down and said, "Hop on!"

Meir carefully and very slowly climbed onto Dovid's shoulders. When he was balanced (and holding Dovid's head tightly - although trying not to hurt him), Dovid got up and carefully stood on his feet.

Then he handed the camera up to Meir, who was trying desperately not to look down as he took the camera from Dovid. Dovid made his way slowly to where the vent was and Meir then began trying to pull off the grate that was covering the vent. During this time, Dovid who wasn't as strong as he thought, was constantly wobbling from side to side.

"Hey! Hold still!" Meir shouted down to him while holding on to the vent hole for dear life!

"Sorry - it's just that you're a little heavy. Could you hurry?" Dovid asked while trying to regain his balance.

Finally Meir managed to put the video camera in place with the lens facing the kitchen. Then he told Dovid to let him come down. Well, that was easier said than done. Dovid's legs were growing tired and his shoulders were aching from Meir's weight. He couldn't stand straight anymore! Poor Meir was terrified of

falling and he began shouting, "Dovid! GET - ME - DOWN!! Help!"

In the meantime, Boruch was laughing so hard watching this that he couldn't even think of helping his friends until Dovid nearly fell, then Boruch ran over and helped to support him while helping Meir get down.

"Are you guys okay?" he asked them as they caught their breath and rested.

"Yeah," they answered breathing heavily.

Dovid then turned to Meir and asked in a soft and kind voice, "Meir, are you okay? I didn't realize you had a fear of heights - I'm sorry."

"That's okay," Meir answered smiling shyly. "I wanted you guys to be proud of me so I didn't tell you."

"Meir," Boruch consoled, "we're always proud of you - and it's okay to have fears in life. You wouldn't be normal if you weren't afraid of anything."

"That's right," Dovid agreed.

"I mean," said Boruch, "I'm terrified of mice, rats and...hamsters!"

The three boys rolled with laughter when Boruch said this, remembering the hamster that scared Boruch in their first mystery.

"And I'm terrified of my neighbor's Rottweiler!" Dovid added. "I'm always having nightmares of that dog waiting for me in my house one day!"

The three boys shuddered at the thought and exclaimed, "*Chas Vesholom*!"

Meir was feeling a lot better when the gang left the kitchen and headed for class.

They agreed to make further plans at lunch break in just a few more hours.

When lunchtime arrived, the boys sat outside on a bench and ate together. They were so excited and nervous about what they would see on the camera that they couldn't wait to surprise the principal, Rabbi Kaplan, when they caught the thief on tape.

Boruch then suddenly turned to his friends and asked, "Hey, do you guys want to sleep over at my house, so we can study and say *Tehillim* together for success?"

"That's an excellent idea!" Dovid exclaimed.

"Yeah," Meir nodded, "we just have to call home to get permission."

So Dovid and Meir used the public phone to call home and Meir's parents, who knew what to expect, agreed to bring over some clothes and things for both Meir and Dovid.

When the gang was involved in mysteries, their parents were understandably always worried at first. But when they felt comfortable enough that the boys would be safe, they let their sons do their "job." They were all very proud of their boys and gave them whatever help and support they could.

After school, the boys were picked up and headed for Boruch's house. When they got there, they immediately sat down to do homework together and study until dinner was ready.

Boruch's mother was also the cook at the Kosher Deli, and boy did she make delicious food! Dinner that night consisted of knishes, schnitzels, vegetable pies and french fries as well as a variety of delicious salads. For dessert they had chocolate ice cream with sprinkles. (As you can imagine, they loved going to Boruch's house as often as they could.)

When dinner was over, the gang went with Boruch's father and older brother to the nearby *Shul*

(Synagogue) to *Daven Ma'ariv* (pray the evening service). When they came home, they sat down to say *Tehillim*. Each boy prayed in his mind for *Hashem* to help them solve the case.

Finally at 11 o'clock, the boys were too exhausted to continue. With Boruch's mother's nudging, they went upstairs and tumbled into bed.

CHAPTER 4 - MEIR AND THE THIEF

The next morning, the gang arrived at school at 6:30 and headed straight for the staff kitchen. This time however, they weren't going to make the same mistake as the last time. They found a step stool that they knew the janitor often used and carried it to the kitchen.

Boruch climbed up onto the stool, pulled out the vent and carefully took out the camera.

"Okay, let's go to one of the empty classrooms and watch it!" Meir shouted excitedly.

The gang then quickly walked over to one of the nearest classrooms and rewound the videotape inside the camera.

Boruch pushed play and they waited. For five minutes there was just fuzz, so Boruch fast-forwarded it while playing. To the boys' horror the whole tape was just fuzz.

"What happened?!" Dovid exclaimed.

"I don't know!" Boruch answered as he opened the camera and began examining the tape.

Meir looked at the front of the camera and asked, "Um, Boruch?"

"Yes," Boruch replied with a very red face as he looked up at Meir.

"What's that button above the lens?" Meir asked while pointing to it.

Boruch looked and said, "That's the record button. Why?"

"Well, when you took down the camera was the button down or up?" Meir asked as Dovid began to understand what must have happened as well.

"It was down," Boruch replied. And then it hit him. "Oh, no! How did that happen?" he moaned.

"I guess that when we put the camera in the vent we must have hit the button and since we weren't looking closely at the lens we didn't realize that the shutter had closed," Meir figured.

"Well, never mind. We'll just do it again tonight! Right?" Dovid asked his friends while trying to cheer them up.

"I guess we have no other choice," Boruch agreed.

"So, come on then, let's go and set it up again," Meir stated. "Is the battery charged enough?"

Boruch checked and saw that there was enough for twenty more hours. "Yep!" He answered gaining hope once again.

The gang then quickly returned to the kitchen, rewound the tape, and set the camera back up in the vent making sure that the shutter of the lens stayed open.

By then, it was time for *Shacharis* (the morning service) down in the school's *shul.* The boys hurried to get there in time for the beginning.

Nothing very interesting happened that morning, just the usual classes, but something *very* interesting happened during lunchtime.

All of the boys in the school were outside playing football and just hanging out during the recess that followed lunch - except for Meir. He had missed some lessons when he was sick, so he stayed after class with his teacher to make them up. When all the other boys went out to play during recess, Meir stayed inside to have his lunch.

He put his sandwich and apple on the table and then went to wash *netilas yadayim.*

While he was out of the classroom, someone in another part of the school was planning something.

Daniel usually took enough food from the kitchen to last for breakfast and lunch the next day but last night the kitchen had been left almost bare. Some teachers forgot to bring their lunches and had emptied the staff kitchen not leaving very much behind. When lunchtime arrived, poor Daniel was famished! He sat thinking for a while about how to get food, until he finally came up with a good, but very risky plan.

Daniel left his room, made sure that the basement was empty, and began searching the supply room for the equipment he would need.

He found a long wire, a mirror (an old car mirror - but it was good enough), a thin pole and amazingly enough - a fishing hook, and put them to use.

One thing that he had learned from living in the basement for so long was that the vent next to the supply room was right under a vent of one of the classrooms. There had been a few times that he had had to sneak out of his secret room to use the basement bathrooms and as he passed the vent he could hear the teacher's and students' voices above very clearly.

First, he took the wire, and on its end he attached the fishing hook. He put this inside the vent hole that to Daniel's relief, was quite large and old-fashioned. Then he removed the vent cover from the vent in the classroom wall above. He then attached the mirror to the pole by using some thick binding tape he was lucky to find and stuck the pole up the vent. By moving the mirror around a bit at different angles he found that he was able to view the classroom.

The classroom was empty and Daniel hit the jackpot! He was hoping that maybe one of the students had left some remnants of their lunch behind, and there, lying on a desk, was an UNTOUCHED sandwich and apple! *Wow!* He thought to himself. *What luck!*

Very carefully, he guided the wire with the hook at the top, up the vent and steered it left into the first row of desks (where Meir sat). Then, using the mirror to guide him, he tried to hook the fishing hook on the bag that contained the sandwich about five times until he finally succeeded. He then pulled the wire very carefully back so the sandwich would fall to the floor, (still attached to the hook of course) and then continued to pull it back towards the vent. Just then, Meir returned. He stood at the entrance of the classroom and stared in horror at his desk - his sandwich was gone! But that was nothing compared to the look on his face when he looked down and saw his sandwich running away and going straight into the vent in the wall!

At first, the terrified Meir couldn't move. Then, when he realized what was happening, he began to run towards the vent to try and save his runaway lunch but he was too late! The sandwich was gone, and Daniel had already taken it to his room so he didn't hear Meir shouting, "Wait! Come back here!"

Meir just sat at his desk in total shock trying to figure out what just happened.

Then it hit him. "The thief!" he exclaimed to himself. "He's just stolen in broad daylight! And he stole *my* lunch!"

Well, fortunately for Meir, the school always carried spare mini cereal boxes for kids who forgot their lunches. He walked over to the supply closet in the corner of the classroom and took out a box of Cornflakes. After getting some milk from the cafeteria and eating his cereal, Meir ran outside to the playground to tell Dovid and Boruch what just happened. The boys couldn't believe their ears.

"I can't believe he would risk stealing in the daytime when he could easily have gotten caught!" Dovid said in shock.

"Yeah!" Boruch added. "Now I really can't wait to catch that thief and solve this strange mystery!"

For the rest of that day, the gang had to work very hard to put the mystery out of their minds and stay focused on their classes. There was one thing to be said about these boys, no matter how excited they were about solving their mysteries they *never* let it interfere with their studies. If anything, they learned harder so that *Hashem* would help them and give them the wisdom they needed to solve mysteries.

CHAPTER 5 – AHARON HELLER

The next morning, Thursday, the gang met at the school once again, and headed for the staff kitchen. They took down the camera and went into their own classroom so that if someone saw them, nothing would look suspicious. Boruch once again rewound the tape to the beginning, praying in his mind that this had worked.

Then he pushed 'play'.

Minutes later, after fast-forwarding a little to 8:30 p.m. Dovid shouted, "Push play! I see a figure!"

The boys watched and couldn't believe their eyes.

"Wow!" Boruch exclaimed. "It's a young kid with a *Yarmulke*!"

"Yeah, I can't believe it!" Meir added, eyes still wide open from shock.

The boys were actually each silently relieved that it was a boy because now they didn't have to be afraid of trying to catch the thief themselves. They weren't quite sure what they would have done if it were an adult. Dovid had figured that if it had been an adult they would have had to leave the rest up to the police. That would have been a bit disappointing since the gang always liked to carry out a job to the finish.

"Does he look familiar at all?" Dovid asked his friends.

"No." Meir replied.

Boruch shook his head and said, "Not at all!"

"I've never seen him around school, so I don't think he learns here," Dovid stated.

The other two shook their heads in agreement as Dovid looked at them and then continued.

"And, since we know that just last week, Rabbi Kaplan had alarms installed on all the windows and doors of the school, there is no way this boy is coming in and out, right?"

Boruch and Meir nodded and understood very well what Dovid was getting at.

"So that can mean only one thing!" Dovid slammed his hand down on the table, as if to get their attention (which he had anyway) and said, "This boy is LIVING IN THE SCHOOL!"

At first, the gang just sat quietly, while each boy pictured in his own mind, a young boy sleeping on a desk? Or maybe on a mat in the sports room? Where was he living?

"How will we find him? I mean," Boruch began, "when the school is full, the boy surely hides somewhere. But it has to be a place that even the janitor doesn't know of."

"That's right, Boruch," Meir agreed. "So, Dovid, what do you think? How *can* we find him?"

"Hmm," Dovid cleared his throat and began rubbing his chin in deep thought.

"Hey!" he suddenly shouted. "I've got it!"

"Well?" Meir and Boruch asked together.

"Aharon Heller!" Dovid explained.

"What about him?" Meir curiously asked.

"His father owns a store for security devices, remember?"

"Yeah!" Boruch excitedly replied for Meir and himself.

"Well," Dovid began while moving his chair closer to his friends. He was getting excited with this brilliant idea which was forming in his mind.

"What if we borrowed some tiny security cameras and set them up on every floor of the school, in different locations. When this boy comes to take food from the kitchen at night, we can watch his moves and

54

see where he goes. He probably DOES have a hiding place and this is the best way for us to find it!"

"Dovid, I always knew you were brilliant!" said Meir standing up and shaking Dovid's hand ferociously, while patting his shoulder with the other hand.

"Great Work!" Boruch added, with a big toothy smile.

"Are you sure Aharon can get the stuff?" Meir then suddenly asked, with doubt in his voice.

"Well, I'm pretty sure. He once told me that every so often his father gives him some old devices that no one wants anymore, for him to 'play' with," Dovid assuredly replied. Then he moved his chair back, got up and said, "I'll go ask him now, okay?"

"Good idea," Meir smiled.

"We'll meet you in *Mishnah* class in ten minutes, let us know what he said, okay?" Boruch asked.

"Sure, see you then!" Dovid ran out and went to look for Aharon, who was a year ahead of the gang in school.

Aharon Heller was a good soul and loved to help people. When Dovid came up to him two minutes later to borrow the little cameras, he immediately replied, "No problem, Dovid. Come over to my house later today and I'll give you all *ten* of my cameras!"

Not only was he happy to help the famous 'Gimmel Gang', but he was glad in his heart to be a part of what would end up being a great Mitzvah.

Dovid thanked him and headed back to class to meet his friends.

"So how did it go?" Boruch asked him nervously.

"Aharon was great! He said, 'sure!'" Dovid happily replied. He then turned quietly and added, while thinking, "Wow, I just realized that he didn't even ask what I needed them for!"

"Now that's what I call a REAL *mensch*." Meir stated. "To help someone without question is a greater *mitzvah* than to help and demand to know why."

The gang smiled and returned to their seats just as Rabbi Gold, the *Mishnah* teacher, entered the classroom.

Later, at 4:30 that afternoon, Dovid was knocking on Aharon Heller's front door. Mr. Heller answered the door and gladly let Dovid in.

When Dovid entered Aharon's room, his eyes opened wide. He couldn't believe what he was seeing. The shelves, desk and even the bed were covered with all kinds of security devices. His father had given him some laser burglar detectors for his last birthday and he didn't really have much use for them, so he set them up all around his desk and shelves.

"This way I always know when my little brother is into my stuff," he proudly explained to Dovid, who couldn't stop gaping and saying "Wow - wow!"

Finally Aharon gave Dovid ten tiny security cameras and a video monitor, and explained how they worked, how to connect them afterwards to the monitor to view them and how to put them up on the walls. He wished Dovid and the gang '*Hatzlacha*' (good luck) and walked Dovid to the nearby bus stop.

The gang could hardly wait until the next Monday to act on their plan.

On Monday morning, the gang met at school half an hour before school started to plan their day.

After each of their four breaks, the boys went around the school and set up the cameras in the hallways on every floor.

At the end of the day, they made sure that all of the cameras were in place, and the gang headed home.

That night, not one of them was able to sleep. They were so nervous and yet excited about what the cameras would reveal to them. They were also terribly curious. Where in the world could that boy be hiding?

CHAPTER 6 – THE LETTER

The boys woke up very early the next morning and met in front of the school playground at 6:30. They knew that the school was always open from 6:00 so that the teachers could come early to prepare, and so that energetic young boys, like themselves, could learn a bit before class.

Boruch was the first to arrive and he warmly greeted his two best friends as they excitedly walked up to him.

"Come on, guys, I can't wait to see the video tapes!" He motioned for them to hurry.

Together they entered the school, trying very hard not to look excited, so as not to arouse anyone's suspicions.

When they were sure that no one was looking, the boys took down the little security cameras from the walls one by one.

When they were finished, they took them into their classroom where the video was set up and they prepared the tapes for viewing.

They decided to work backwards, and to watch the boy from the time he left the kitchen, and follow him to see where he went.

Suddenly, they all moved in closer to watch the film when they finally reached the part on the video showing the boy in the kitchen. After noting the time, they were able to figure out his steps on the other cameras. After leaving the kitchen, they watched him go down the hallway of the second floor. He then took the stairs down to the first floor and walked through a few halls.

The gang thought they lost him for a minute, but then Boruch spotted him on one of the other cameras, going down the backstairs to the enormous school basement.

"I knew it!" Meir suddenly shouted excitedly causing his friends to jump.

"Well, it's a good thing that we set up cameras down there, as well, huh?" Boruch asked.

"Yep!" Dovid answered, not taking his eyes off of the basement cameras as they continued playing back the tapes.

"Hey! What's he doing?" Meir suddenly asked as he looked at one of the cameras that was showing the supply room.

"Sh-h-h-h! Wait and see." Dovid whispered as if the thief could hear them.

Daniel was moving aside a large stack of shelves filled with paints, markers and other such art supplies.

"*Whoa!* There's a door there!" Boruch exclaimed in surprise.

"It's a secret door!" Dovid added, his eyes opening wider and wider as Daniel unlocked and opened the door to his secret 'home'.

"What's behind that door?" Meir asked while trying to get a better look.

"I don't know," Dovid began to panic. The cameras weren't focused on that section of basement.

"It doesn't matter - at least we know where he is." Boruch intelligently pointed out.

"I guess," Dovid agreed although he wanted to know what was behind that door! He really didn't like surprises.

Now that they knew how to find the boy, the three friends planned to meet in the staff kitchen at the end of the day. They were going to try and find this mysterious boy.

The day dragged on and the boys felt like it would never end. Finally 4:00 showed on their watches, and not a minute too soon.

As planned, the gang met in the kitchen. They waited until they were sure that the halls were empty and then quickly walked towards the staircase. Down to the second floor they went and then on to the back stairs just as Daniel had done every night for the past two months.

When they arrived at the basement entrance, they began to slow down and walk with extra caution. Dovid told them to tiptoe and not to turn on any lights, just in case the boy was outside his secret place.

In the dingy light, they saw shelves filled with art supplies as well as all sorts of things that they would not expect to find in a school. Broken lamps, chairs, telephones and even a cracked chest of drawers were piled up in one corner. Another corner contained a pyramid of rainbow colored paint cans as well as an assortment of rusty tools. It seemed as though no-one ever bothered to straighten up the basement in the 20 years of the school's history. Wow! What a collection of stuff!

Boruch and Meir followed behind Dovid, though not too closely. Suddenly, Boruch tripped over a hammer that was lying on the floor and knocked into Meir who was in front of him, causing him to lose his balance and fall down.

Dovid quickly stopped and looked back to see if Meir was okay. When they signaled to him that they were fine he whispered for them to be careful and to keep quiet.

The boys held their breath and didn't move for what felt like ages. When a few minutes passed and nothing happened, they were relieved that no one seemed to have heard them. *Boruch Hashem!*

Dovid and Meir then began to quietly look about the room until Meir found the shelves that contained all of the different art supplies.

He signaled to Boruch and Dovid who came right over and began to help him push aside the shelves. Very slowly and as quietly as they could, they moved the stack of shelves over to the side until most of the secret door was revealed. The boys, who stopped to rest, looked at the door and smiled to each other. There in front of them stood the entrance to the boy's hideout.

Boruch leaned over to Dovid and whispered, "Now what?"

Dovid was busy thinking about their next step. *We can't really just knock, can we?* he thought. *There might be another door in there leading to the outside and the boy might panic and run away...* But then he had an idea that he hoped would work.

He signaled to his friends to move back and hide behind some shelves nearby. When they were hidden,

Dovid inspected the art supply shelves and found what he was looking for. He took a pen and a colored paper and wrote a short letter.

Hi,

My name is Dovid and I am a student in this school. I have two friends here with me, Meir and Boruch. Don't worry! We're the only ones who know you're here. We are worried about you and thought that you might be hiding here because you are in some kind of trouble. We would like to help you. If you open the door, we could talk and hopefully become friends. We're waiting out here for your answer.

Dovid

Dovid looked over at his friends, winked at them and then slid the note under Daniel's door. When it was

under the door, he quickly went to hide behind some shelves across from where Meir and Boruch were hiding.

CHAPTER 7 – THE GANG MEETS DANIEL

Daniel was sitting at his desk, learning, when all of a sudden he saw a piece of paper being slid under his door.

"What?!" Daniel exclaimed jumping up off of his chair in fear. "Someone knows I'm here! What am I going to do?" Daniel found that he was so afraid he was shaking all over and beginning to sweat on his brow. *"I'll run away"*, he thought. *"Wait, I can't. There's no way out of here. Maybe I'll just sit quietly and they'll think I'm not here and go away."* But somehow he was sure that whoever had put that note there, knew that he was inside. That's when he realized that the person couldn't be mean or dangerous because otherwise he would have broken down that rusty old door.

Suddenly Daniel became a little hopeful. Maybe *Hashem* sent this person. Maybe this person was sent to help him! Very slowly and cautiously, he walked over to the door and picked up the note. He unfolded it and sat down to read it.

When he finished reading the letter, Daniel just sat quietly holding it in his hand, not moving a muscle.

Can I trust these people? he wondered. *How do I know that they won't turn me in to the police?*

These questions were repeating themselves in his mind over and over and yet, his gut feeling was that he could trust these boys.

Daniel made up his mind and went to open his door. But when he looked out into the basement, there was no one there! Daniel's heart actually sank, but as he turned to go back inside, Dovid suddenly jumped out from behind the shelves. He had been so deep in thought that he hadn't noticed Daniel opening his door. But when he did, Dovid jumped so suddenly that he scared Daniel who stumbled back, tripped and fell! "Ouch!" Daniel exclaimed in pain.

"Oh! Are you okay?" Dovid asked as he rushed over to help. Daniel gratefully took his outstretched hand and pulled himself up.

"Yeah, I'm okay. You just startled me," Daniel mumbled in embarrassment.

"I'm really sorry! I was so lost in thought, wondering if you were ever going to come out or not, that I didn't notice you opening your door and..." Dovid was rushing to explain when he suddenly stopped. He was finally taking in the sight of Daniel and just couldn't speak anymore. Daniel had grown very thin over the past two months, had long hair and smelled heavily of old musty furniture. Daniel actually did try to wash himself with the soap in the school bathrooms at night, but as soon as he returned to his room he would once again take on the smell of his surroundings.

Dovid felt tears fill his eyes as he examined poor Daniel from head to toe and realized that this was no ordinary thief, but rather a young Jewish boy, like himself, in need of help. The tears caught in his throat and he couldn't speak. He then swallowed hard a couple of times and said, "Hi. I'm Dovid." He turned around and signaled for Meir and Boruch to join him.

The two boys came out from behind the shelves and introduced themselves. They couldn't stop staring at Daniel and wondering how he ended up in this place.

Daniel looked at them and smiled.

"I wish I could tell you who I am but, I don't know," he mumbled sadly.

"How can you not know?" Dovid asked, confused.

"Well, why don't you guys come in and I'll tell you my story," Daniel said as he backed into the room to let the gang enter.

"Wow!" the gang said together as they looked around the secret room. Daniel had the friends sit

together on the shabby old sofa that he had been using as his bed, while he himself took a seat on an old chair.

Not knowing quite what to say, but wanting to be polite, Boruch stammered with an uneasy smile, "N-nice place you have here."

Daniel raised his eyebrows as if to say, "Are you kidding me?" and the four boys burst out laughing.

"Boy," said Daniel when he calmed down from laughing so hard but was still grinning widely, "I don't know how long it's been since I've laughed, but it sure feels good!"

The gang smiled sadly at this and Meir said, "So, tell us your story. How in the world did you end up living here?"

For the next thirty minutes, Daniel told the gang of all that happened since he woke up a bit more than two months before in the entrance of a building site that had collapsed as he walked by it.

75

"So you see," he sighed sadly. "This is why I've needed to take food from the kitchen upstairs every night, and the books I took to keep up with my learning. I'm just so afraid that if I go to the police, I'll end up in a non-Jewish home and who knows what could happen then."

The gang understood everything now and realized that they couldn't tell the police or Rabbi Kaplan about Daniel until they figured out what to do. They had to make sure that Daniel would end up in a Jewish home.

After a few minutes of silence, Dovid suddenly sat upright and said, "Daniel, you can't keep living in this place anymore!" He was pointing to the room surrounding them. "It's unhealthy and you need to gain weight before you end up in the hospital!"

Daniel looked back at Dovid with such sad eyes and said, "What choice do I have?"

Dovid stood up, opened the door and said, "I'll be right back, guys!" And before anyone could protest he was gone.

Five minutes later, Dovid returned and said in a very matter-of-fact voice, "You're coming to sleep over at my house."

Daniel looked up with hopeful eyes and said, "Really? But..."

"Don't worry," Dovid reassured him knowing what the scared boy was thinking. "For now, the only thing I have told my parents is that I'm bringing over a new friend. But you can trust my parents, they won't turn you in and if anything they'll want to help you."

"Are you sure?" Daniel asked. He was glad to be able to leave this place but he was also afraid. This room may be musty and smelly but to him it was home and he felt safe in it. What would the future hold for him now in the outside world?

"One hundred percent!" Dovid answered with a huge grin.

"Well," Daniel hesitated for a moment before saying, "okay."

"Great! Let's go!" Dovid said happily as he went to exit the still-open door. And then he realized something; "Uh-Daniel," he said.

"Yes?" Daniel asked afraid that Dovid may have changed his mind. "You should probably wear a hat or people might suspect something."

Daniel felt his hair and realized Dovid was right. "Have you got one?"

Meir who had been sitting quietly with Boruch still in shock from the whole thing piped up and said, "I have one in my bag!" He reached into the big pocket of his knapsack and pulled out a Denver Broncos football cap and placed it on Daniel's head.

"You can keep it as a souvenir from me," he added kindly.

"Wow, thanks Meir!" Daniel said, touched.

The four boys headed out when Dovid stopped and added one more thing.

"Oh!" he began. "I forgot something else. Meir and Boruch, you're also sleeping over!"

"Whew! We thought you'd never ask!" Meir and Boruch answered with relief.

CHAPTER 8 – THE FREEDMANS

Half an hour later, Dovid's parents came to the school with their Dodge mini-van and picked up the four boys. When they got into the car, Mrs. Freedman said, "What's that musty smell?" She couldn't imagine that one of the boys smelled that way or she wouldn't have said anything. When the boys shrugged she just figured that one of them probably had some old food that had gone bad in their bags. Dovid looked over at Daniel and winked, as he mouthed *"Don't worry."*

When they arrived at Dovid's house, the first thing Daniel asked to do was to take a shower.

"Sure," said Dovid as he led Daniel to the bathroom. He gave him a clean towel and some of his own clothes to wear. Daniel was a little shorter than him, so Dovid tried to find him some clothes that were a bit small on him. Daniel thanked Dovid warmly and went into the bathroom closing the door behind him.

When Dovid had returned downstairs, his mother and father were waiting for him in the living room.

"Uh," Dovid stammered when he saw the suspicious looks on their faces. "Mommy, Daddy, can I speak with you both privately for a minute?"

It wasn't every day that Dovid brought home a very unnaturally thin boy who smelled of old furniture and who desperately needed a haircut (his hat wasn't big enough to hide the length of his hair). They were waiting for some sort of an explanation.

"Sure Dovid, let's go into the study," Dovid's parents said curiously. They led Dovid to the room where Dr. Freedman worked and learned when he was at home.

When Dovid and his parents were sitting down, Dovid explained the whole story, starting with the gang overhearing Rabbi Kaplan speak about the thefts to finding Daniel in the secret room that very afternoon.

Dovid's parents stared at him as if he had just told them that an alien had landed on their doorstep.

"Wow!" Dr. Freedman said when he found his voice. "The poor boy!"

"Yeah!" said Mrs. Freedman nodding her head in agreement. "Yet, something about this story and this boy sounds familiar, but I'm not sure why." She put her hand to her forehead as if to help her to try and think what was familiar about this. After a few minutes, though, nothing came to mind so she said, "Dovid, let your father and I speak with each other for a moment and we'll let you know what we think when we're done, okay?"

Dovid nodded as he left the room closing the door behind him.

Just then, Daniel came down the steps looking and feeling (and smelling) much better than he had in two months. Together they returned to where the others were nervously waiting to hear what happened. Dovid told Daniel not to worry, his parents would find a way to help.

What seemed like ages later, Dovid's parents finally came out of the study and had very serious looks on their faces.

"Okay," Mrs. Freedman began as she sat down on the rocking chair facing the sofa, "We know how much you boys want to solve this mystery on your own."

The gang nodded their heads as she continued.

"So, we'll give you kids a week to find out the boy's name."

"But," Dovid protested only to quiet down again with one look from his father.

Dovid apologized for interrupting and let his mother continue.

"Now, after one week, if you don't find out who the boy's parents are, we will have to go to the police."

Daniel's head dropped to his chest just as Mrs. Freedman added one more thing.

"If the police can't find your parents either," she said looking at Daniel, "then you are welcome to stay here for as long as you would like, if you want of course."

"Huh?" the four boys asked together not believing what they just heard.

"I am?" Daniel stammered. "B-but you don't even know me!" he added pointing out the obvious.

Dr. Freedman heard this and thought *"What a special boy. Instead of worrying that he won't like us, he's afraid that we won't like him!"* He smiled down at Daniel and said, "Yes, you are."

Dovid ran up to his parents and threw his arms around them in embrace. "You are the best parents!" he shouted excitedly making his parents laugh shyly. "Thanks!"

Daniel was red in the face and didn't know what to say. "That's really nice of you," he whispered bashfully.

"Okay kids," Dr. Freedman said as Dovid moved back to join his friends. "You've got some work to do, right?"

"Yeah! Let's get started!" Meir answered for the gang while jumping up off of the sofa with joy.

The gang then led Daniel into the study, which became one of their meeting places in the days to follow.

"All right," Boruch began the meeting. "Let's think. Where should we start?"

"Hmm," Dovid replied. "Let's just sit quietly and think to ourselves for a few minutes until someone comes up with an idea."

The four boys sat quietly for about ten minutes when Meir suddenly sat upright and said, "I think I have an idea."

When all eyes were on him, he went on to explain, "I think we should start with newspapers. I mean, think about it. If a Jewish boy disappeared in Denver or somewhere around here, surely it would be on the news, right?"

"Probably," Boruch said as the others were seeing the logic in this as well.

"And," Meir continued, "Since it was a *Jewish* boy who disappeared, it probably would have been in the Jewish newspaper, right?"

"Yeah, that makes sense," Dovid agreed.

"Okay. Now, it happened in the summer, right?" Meir asked Daniel.

"Yes," Daniel replied, feeling even more hopeful than before. *These boys are really good at this,* he thought to himself excitedly. *If anyone can help me, they can!*

"So, all we need are the Jewish newspapers from last summer," Meir concluded.

"How are we going to get them without arousing any suspicion?" Dovid asked. "If we phone the Jewish newspaper asking for any editions concerning a boy who disappeared, they'll think that we know something and someone might tell the police!"

"Hey! I know how we can get the papers!" Boruch suddenly exclaimed.

"How?" Daniel asked. He wanted to help anyway he could.

"My grandmother saves all of the Jewish newspapers," Boruch explained.

"She does?" Dovid asked surprised. But when he thought his surprise may have sounded offensive he quickly said "I mean, that's great! Can you get the summer ones from her tomorrow?"

"Well, you know, she also has a fax machine and a computer which we could use if we should need them, so why don't we *all* go over there?"

"That's a good idea," said Dovid.

"I'm all for it!" Meir agreed, smiling.

CHAPTER 9 – MYSTERY SOLVED

Daniel spent the rest of the evening with the gang, eating dinner, going to *shul* to *daven Maariv*, studying together and even having a bit of fun, too.

The next day was a teacher's workshop day so there was no school. At six o'clock the next morning, after the four boys got dressed and ready, they went to the nearest *shul* to *daven Shacharis*.

They returned to the Freedmans' house at eight and sat right down to have breakfast. Daniel, of course, was especially enjoying the food. He had grown pretty tired of bread and cream cheese. Pancakes were a welcome change!

After breakfast, Dovid's mother gave the boys a ride to Boruch's grandmother, 'Bubby Kahns' house. Bubby Kahn was delighted to see the boys. She led them into the living room where on the table were stacks of past Jewish newspapers.

Daniel had disappeared in the second week of July, so the kids began looking at the papers with the July dates.

For about half an hour, the boys scanned the newspapers until Daniel himself let out a yelp of excitement.

"What is it?" Boruch asked.

"Did you find something?" Meir added as he came around the coffee table to sit by Daniel.

"Yes and no," Daniel said. Then he showed them what he meant. "I found an article about a boy who disappeared in July, but the picture is so badly smudged that I can't tell if it's me or not!"

Bubby Kahn heard this and said, "What? Let me see that."

She usually took such good care of her papers but when she saw the smudge she realized what it was.

"Oh dear," she said sadly. "That's when Uncle Aryeh was visiting one *Shabbos* and spilled coffee all over the newspaper."

The gang gathered around Daniel to look at the article and agreed that the picture was really too smudged to see.

"What can we do?" Daniel asked the gang.

"Hmm," Dovid thought out loud for a minute. "How can we get a clear picture?"

"I'll bet the police have a clear picture but they wouldn't show it to a bunch of *kids*..." Meir intelligently pointed out.

Just then Boruch jumped up and said, "I know who would!"

"Who?" the others asked in unison.

"OFFICER WARNER!" Boruch excitedly replied.

"Oh, Yeah! What a good idea!" Dovid and Meir exclaimed.

Officer Warner was the nice policeman who had helped the gang in their first mystery. If there was anyone they could count on, it was good old Officer Dan Warner.

The next thing the boys knew, Boruch ran to the phone (after getting permission from Bubby) and called the Denver Police Station.

"Hello? May I speak with Officer Warner?" the others heard him say.

After a brief wait, Boruch explained the whole story to Officer Warner who promised not to tell anyone just yet.

The Officer really admired these young boys and was always prepared to help them.

"Sure, Boruch!" he was saying. "I can stop by your grandmother's house in about an hour with the picture of Daniel Rubin, the boy who disappeared last summer."

"Thanks a lot!" Boruch finished. "See you soon!"

The four boys used that hour to enjoy a delicious lunch prepared by Bubby Kahn.

Daniel found that he was so nervous that he was eating very quickly as if that would make the hour go by faster. When Bubby Kahn pointed out that he would just get indigestion from eating so fast, he calmed himself down and slowed his eating as well.

One hour and nine minutes later, there was a knock on the door.

"I'll get it!" The gang shouted all at once jumping up out of their chairs. They giggled as together they went to open the door and greet Officer Warner.

"Hi guys!" He cheerfully greeted them back. "How have you been?"

"Great, thanks!" the gang answered.

Daniel was still sitting unnoticed in the kitchen when Officer Warner took out the photograph to show to the boys.

"Wow!" Dovid exclaimed. "It *is* him!"

"Really?" Daniel gasped as he ran over to take a look.

Well, Daniel was quite a bit thinner now but there was no mistake. It was Daniel all right.

"*Boruch Hashem*," he whispered, still in shock.

"Hey, you're the kid!" Officer Warner exclaimed while studying Daniel. "Way to go, guys! You found the missing kid!"

The gang smiled up at him and then at Daniel, who was too overwhelmed to talk.

Meir walked up to Daniel and said, "Nice to meet you, Daniel Rubin."

Daniel, not quite knowing what to say looked up at his newly found friend with tears of joy in his eyes and smiled. Then he began to giggle! And all of a sudden all four boys were laughing together from joy.

"Let's go tell my parents!" Dovid said. *"And they thought it would take us a week*!" he added laughing at how quickly they were able to solve this mystery.

The gang and Daniel thanked Officer Warner who said he was just glad he could help. He offered to give the boys a ride to Dovid's house and the boys gladly took him up on it.

When they arrived at Dovid's house, Dovid ran inside to tell his parents of the good news.

"Wow! You're kidding!" were their remarks when they heard who Daniel was. Mrs. Freedman then suddenly burst out with, "I *knew* there was something familiar about him!" She remembered now having seen that article last summer.

"Daniel," Dr. Freedman said, glad that he could call the boy by his name now. "If you don't mind, I would like to call your parents now. This is something that needs to be done very delicately, if you know what I mean. They probably thought that they would never see you again," he explained heading towards the kitchen to make the phone call. Daniel nodded his head in approval.

A minute later, the operator was putting Dr. Freedman through to the Rubins in Cleveland.

"Uh, Hello?" he began softly. "Mr. and Mrs. Rubin? Um, I'm calling to give you some good news. Are you sitting down?"

CHAPTER 10 – THE REUNION

After Dr. Freedman told the Rubins that it seemed some young boys may have found their son, all at once the Rubins were crying and laughing at the same time. They couldn't believe their good fortune!

"*Boruch Hashem*! *Boruch Hashem*! (Thank Hashem)" they kept saying over and over. When they calmed down a bit, Dr. Freedman told them the whole story starting from when Daniel disappeared.

"It's a *ness* (miracle)!" Mrs. Rubin said. "But has his memory returned? Does he remember us?" she suddenly asked in a worried voice.

"Um, I'm afraid not," Dr. Freedman said sadly. "But I would like to try something before you both arrive here this evening to pick him up.

"Yes? What?" they asked curiously.

Dovid's father was a doctor and had some experience with memory loss. "Do you have e-mail?" he asked.

"Sure," they replied.

"Great!" Dr. Freedman continued. "Now, do you by any chance have a scanner or scanned pictures of you and your home on a file in your computer?"

"Well, I have a digital camera downstairs in my office so I can take some instant pictures!" Mr. Rubin answered happily. He was beginning to see Dr. Freedman's idea.

"Good. Maybe you could take some pictures of Daniel's room, the two of you and anything else you think might jog his memory. Then, you can send it to my e-mail address."

They ended the phone call and immediately reserved seats on a flight to Denver that same evening. The Rubins hurried to take pictures and send them to

Dr. Freedman's E-mail address, praying that his idea would work.

As soon as the photos arrived, Dr. Freedman called Daniel into the study to show him the pictures. One by one he showed them to Daniel, but nothing, not even his parents, looked familiar.

Dovid's father sadly called Daniel's parents.

"I'm sorry, but it didn't work. Can you think of anything that was special to Daniel that might bring his memory back?" he asked.

"Hmm," Mrs. Rubin thought for a minute and said, "We'll think about it and let you know."

Ten minutes later, the Rubins sent photos of things that were special to Daniel. His model plane given to him by his grandfather, and his little Torah from his mother, but these things didn't look at all familiar to Daniel. He was starting to lose hope of ever remembering who he was.

Just before their flight was to leave, while the Rubins were still checking in at the airport, an idea suddenly came to Mrs. Rubin.

"I'll be right back!" she said quickly to Mr. Rubin as she ran off to find the nearest pay phone.

A moment later the phone rang at the Freedman's house.

"Hello?" Mrs. Freedman answered.

The two women had a very interesting conversation for a few minutes and then hung up.

Mrs. Freedman came out of the kitchen, smiling broadly to herself and asked the family not to come into the kitchen for the next two hours. She figured that this would give her plenty of time to do what she needed to do.

"Okay," they all answered, as they exchanged bewildered looks. They had never been more curious about what was going on.

Two hours later, the four boys all went to *shul* to *daven Maariv*. When they returned to Dovid's house, they decided to stay near the living room windows so they could look out and watch for Daniel's parents. No sooner had Daniel gone to look out of the window when he suddenly stood very still. He began sniffing, again and again like a puppy dog.

"Daniel? Are you okay?" Boruch asked him.

Daniel just stood there with a dreamy look on his face.

"Mmm," he said. "Chocolate chip cookies. My favorite!"

Then, as if lightning had struck him, Daniel

suddenly charged into the kitchen and ran straight to

the oven where he opened the oven door and opened his eyes wide.

"Mom!" he shouted. "You made my favorite!"

Then he whipped around expecting to find his dear mother standing there and was shocked to see Mrs. Freedman and the gang staring at him.

Mrs. Freedman was the only one smiling.

The gang, on the other hand, still didn't understand and didn't know what to say. *What's going on?* they wondered.

Just then the doorbell rang bringing everyone's attention back to the present.

"Mom!" Daniel exclaimed and ran to open the front door.

He opened the door and fell into his mother's arms.

It worked! she thought to herself holding her dearest and only son tightly as tears streamed down her cheeks.

"Oh, my Daniel!" she cried.

Daniel then hugged his father tightly and they all entered Dovid's home.

For the next hour, until supper was ready, Daniel and his parents were left alone in a room to catch up on all that happened and to spend some time together. The three united people could not stop thanking *Hashem* for their good fortune.

Everyone had a nice time around the supper table, talking and laughing together and enjoying the special meal that Mrs. Freedman prepared.

When the meal was over, Mrs. Freedman hurried into the kitchen and returned a moment later with an enormous tray of chocolate chip cookies. As soon as Mrs. Rubin saw this, she burst out laughing which caused everyone to stop talking and look over in her direction. When Mr. Rubin and Daniel saw what was in the tray, they joined Mrs. Rubin (and now Mrs. Freedman as well) in the laughter. Daniel then explained to the gang and the Freedmans how much he'd always loved his mother's chocolate chip cookies and amazingly, the smell of them earlier, had brought back his memory.

"Wow!" Meir exclaimed. "*Hashem* really does work in mysterious ways!"

When the laughter had died down, Mr. Rubin stood up and asked to make an announcement.

"First of all, I'd like to thank *Hashem* for sending the Gimmel Gang and the Freedmans to save our only son, Daniel," he began while smiling (yet with tears in his eyes) at everyone.

"I'd also like to make an announcement that will surprise everyone here, even my wife."

He smiled to himself as he thought how happy she would be when she heard what he had to say.

"Last week, I was offered a very good job here in Denver. My wife, who loves the Jewish community here, very much wanted to come, (mostly because she hoped we would find Daniel again one day) but I wasn't really sure that I wanted to. Well, I've just made up my mind." He looked down at Daniel and said, "Daniel, would it be okay with you if we moved to Denver?"

All at once, the gang started whispering loudly, "Yes! Yes! Move here, move here!"

Daniel smiled at his new friends, looked up at his father and said, "You bet it would!"

Everyone at the table then applauded and laughed. They were all so excited about this decision.

When no one else was looking, Mrs. Rubin mouthed *thank you* to her husband with tears in her eyes. She was even more excited than before about moving to Denver. Now she knew what nice people lived there.

At ten-thirty, everyone said their good byes and Daniel hugged his friends, thanking them again. "You guys saved my life, I'll never forget that."

The gang blushed and smiled as they waved good bye (for now) to the Rubins.

Mrs. Rubin turned back and said to Mrs. Freedman, "I just want you to know that if *Chas Vesholom* (Heaven forbid) Daniel would have never found us, you would have been my family of choice to look after him." She hugged Dovid's mother and added, "Thank you, thank you for everything."

"It was our pleasure. He's such a nice boy!" Mrs. Freedman replied.

The End

Epilogue

Two weeks later, the gang was sitting in class when a very excited Rabbi Kaplan walked in.

"Boys," he announced. "We have a new student who has come to join your class and I'd like you all to make him feel welcome. His name is Daniel Rubin and he just moved here yesterday from Cleveland, Ohio."

Daniel walked in and the class began clapping. They had all heard about the missing child and admired his courage for the way he chose to live in order to keep his faith in Judaism. When the clapping died down, the gang signaled for Daniel to come and sit with them at their table.

Soon enough Daniel became pretty popular, as the gang's latest mystery was known to all.

The gang, of course remained modest and looked forward to their next mystery.

Look for more adventures of the

'GIMMEL GANG' coming soon.

Next in the Gimmel Gang series...

The Gimmel Gang and their families take a trip to Israel. The boys get separated from the family and in the process, stumble upon a secret cave.

What happens?

Don't miss the next exciting adventures of the Gimmel Gang in **"The Cave"**.

More in the Gimmel Gang series...